My Car by Byron Barton

Greenwillow Books, *An Imprint of HarperCollinsPublishers*

My Car. Copyright © 2001 by Byron Barton. All rights reserved. Printed in Singapore by Tien Wah Press. www.harperchildrens.com   The full-color art was created in Adobe Photoshop™. The text type is Avant Garde Gothic.   Library of Congress Cataloging-in-Publication Data: Barton, Byron. My car / written and illustrated by Byron Barton.   p.   cm. "Greenwillow Books."   Summary: Sam describes in loving detail his car and how he drives it.   ISBN 0-06-029624-0 (trade).   ISBN 0-06-029625-9 (lib. bdg.)   [1. Automobiles—Fiction.] I. Title.   PZ7.B2848 My 2001   [E]—dc21   00-050334
1 2 3 4 5 6 7 8 9 10   First Edition

I am
Sam.

This
is
my
car.

I love
my
car.

I
keep
my
car
clean.

My
car
needs
oil

and a full tank

of gasoline.

My car has many parts.

body

steering
wheel

engine

wheel

frame

wheel

My
car
has
lights
to
see
at
night

and windshield wipers

to see in the rain.

When I drive,

I drive carefully.

the laws.

I stop

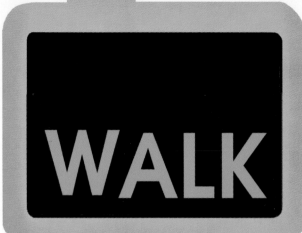

WALK

for pedestrians.

BUS

MAIN ST

ONE WAY

NO PARKING

I
read
the
signs.

I
drive
my
car
to
many
places.

I drive my car to work.

But
when
I work,

BUS

I drive

my bus.